Papa's Wild Child

Dianna Hutts Aston

Illustrated by Nora Hilb

ini Charlesbridge

Thousands of emperor penguin fathers and chicks huddle together for warmth in their rookery.

If I were your penguin papa and you were my chick,
   I would search the rookery
   for the friendliest penguin papa.
Then, as the sun circled the sky,
   he and I would waddle away the hours,
   while you and his chick played
   peekaboo and hide-and-seek.

If I were your swan papa and you were my cygnet,
I would lead you across the lake,
and if you were cold or tired,
I would let you ride on my back,
between my wings,
where it is soft and safe.

A mute swan father will take the first hatchling to the water while the mother keeps the nest of eggs warm.

If I were your fish papa and you were my fry,
I would tuck you into my mouth
whenever you swam too far away,
and then I would *spit-tooey* you back
into our nest of waterweeds
with your brothers and sisters.

A stickleback father guards his babies
for a week after birth.

If I were your ostrich papa and you were my chick,
I would teach you,
my two-toed wonder-chick,
how to kick, claw, and yell—*boo-oh!*—
so the hyena, the leopard, and the lion
would tremble at the sight of you.

The black-feathered ostrich father guards his nest of eggs at night, while the earth-colored ostrich mother guards by day.

If I were your wolf papa and you were my pup,
I would chase you, race you,
nip, nuzzle, and lick you,
and then we would raise our muzzles and howl
aroooooooooooooooooo!
because we belong together.

After a pup has been weaned from its mother's milk,
it gets meat from its father, who regurgitates part of his own meal.

If I were your sea horse papa and you were my fry,
I would hold fast to the brightest branch of coral
while I carried you in my pouch,
belly dancing beneath a watery sky
until you were ready
to swim free.

A sea horse father can finish giving birth to up to 1,500 fry in the morning and become pregnant again by evening.

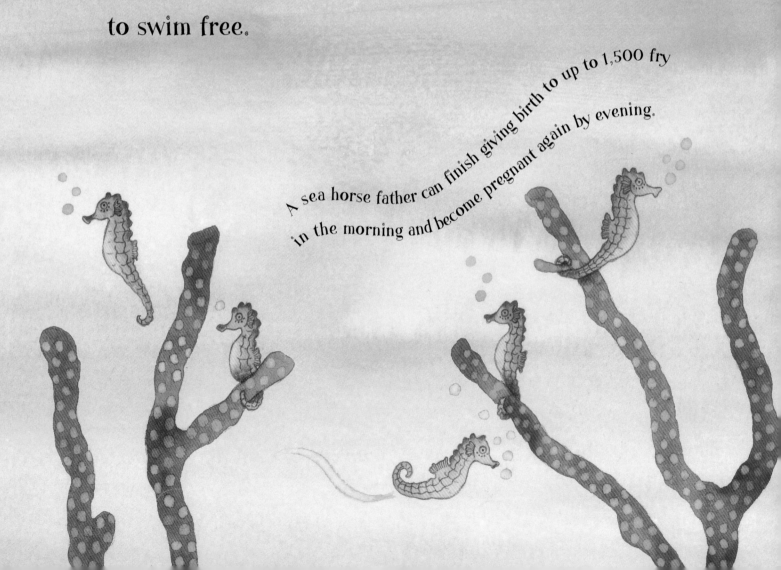

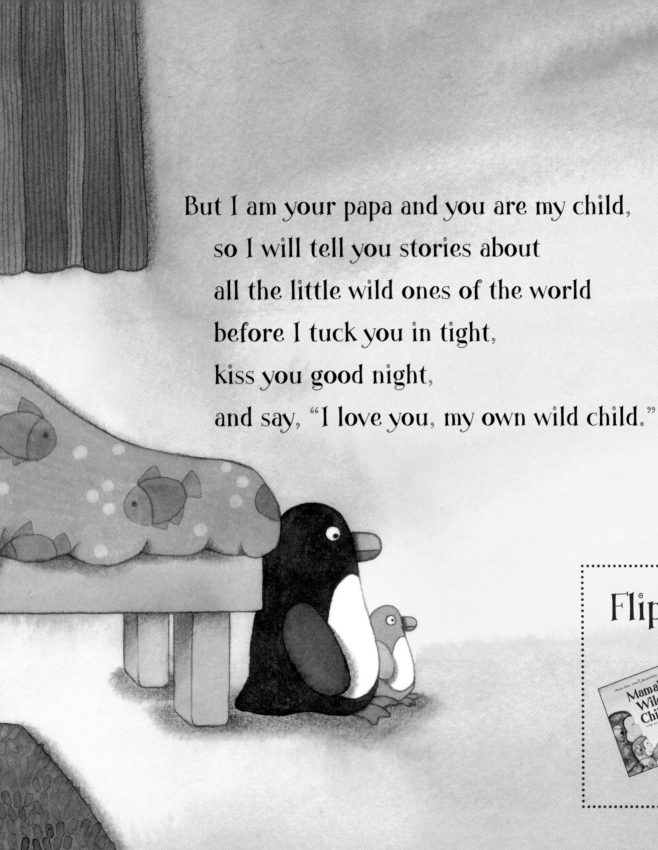

But I am your papa and you are my child,
so I will tell you stories about
all the little wild ones of the world
before I tuck you in tight,
kiss you good night,
and say, "I love you, my own wild child."

Flip me!

Mama's
Wild
Child

But I am your mama and you are my child,
so I will tell you stories about
all the little wild ones of the world
before I tuck you in tight,
kiss you good night,
and say, "I love you, my own wild child."

Flip me!

If I were your crocodile mama and you were my hatchling,
 I would listen for your first *peep-peep-peep*,
 then ferry you gently in my smile
 to your home in the water,
 where you could fill your belly
 with insects, worms, and fish.

A crocodile mother will roll an egg gently back and forth over her tongue if it needs help hatching.

A mother kangaroo has a pouch for the safety and comfort of her young.

If I were your kangaroo mama and you were my joey,
I would tuck you into my pouch
during pouring rains,
and when the clouds rolled away,
I would tap-tap-tap your little head,
and we would hop-in-the-mud, hop-in-the-mud,
hop-in-the-mud.

If I were your llama mama and you were my cria,
I would welcome you into the world
with a big sniff to your woolly head
and then stand by, humming with pride,
as all the other llama mamas
came by to greet you.

A llama mother communicates by humming.

A mother humpback gently pushes her newborn calf to the surface for its first breath of air.

If I were your whale mama and you were my calf,

I would give you a piggyback ride,

up, up, up,

and we would *blo-o-o-o-o-ow!*

Then we would splish-splash with flippers and flukes

on the sunny side of the ocean.

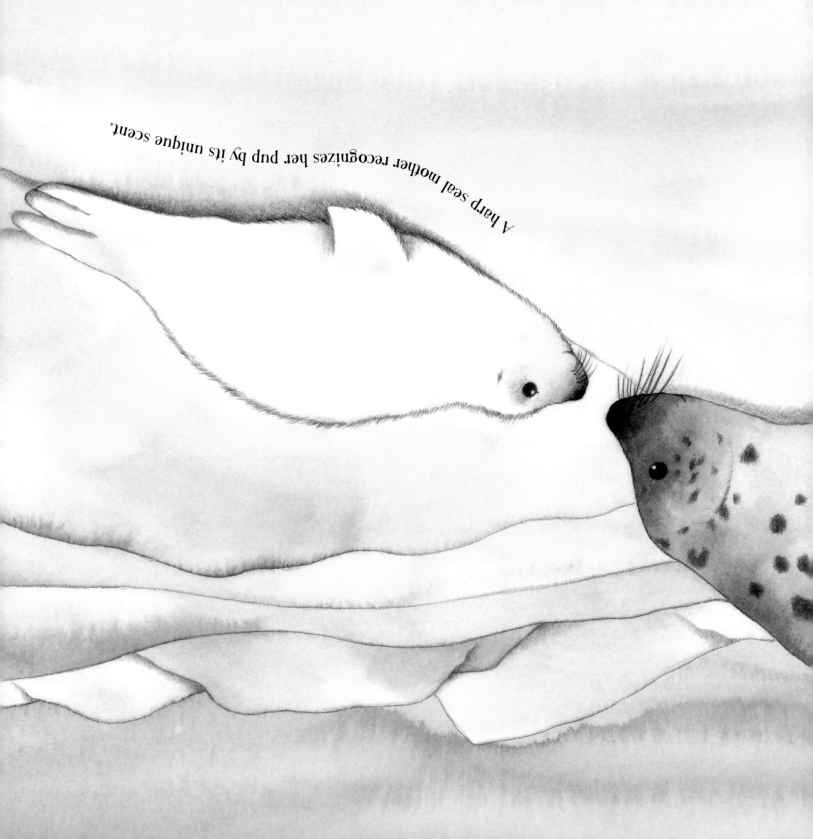

A harp seal mother recognizes her pup by its unique scent.

If I were your seal mama and you were my pup,
   I would breathe in the sweet smell of you.
Whenever you cried *maa, maa . . .*
   I would flip-flop-*sli-i-i-i-de* to your side,
   and we would cuddle together
   in a cradle of ice.

If I were your chimpanzee mama and you were my chimp,
we would knuckle-walk in the jungle sun.
When the stars came out,
I would build us a sleeping platform
so we could rock-a-bye in the treetops,
listening to the lullaby of leaves.

Each day a chimp mother builds a fresh bed of leaves for herself and her baby.